A Little Book of
Tarot Tales

DIANE KING

Beaten Track
www.beatentrackpublishing.com

A Little Book of Tarot Tales
First Published 2022 by Beaten Track Publishing
Copyright 2022 Diane King

All rights reserved.

Paperback ISBN: 978 1 78645 543 7
eBook ISBN: 978 1 78645 544 4

Illustrations: Maryna Yakovchuk

The Entwined; Angel Boy; True Love; Forever:
inspired by The Witches' Wisdom Tarot

Elemental; Wild Child; Dilemma; Persistence, or the Cost
of Peace: inspired by the Dark Wood Tarot

The Path; Acroterium: inspired by
the Forest of Enchantment Tarot

Beaten Track Publishing,
Burscough, Lancashire.
www.beatentrackpublishing.com

Contents

The Entwined

SIX OF FIRE

The baked earth, scorched dry, holds the flames deep within its belly. Only the bold remain on the arid surface, basking in the bare bones of fire.

The mild will wilt; the soft will scorch; those emblazoned with thorns and scales will thrive.

Magic manifests when two of the same skin entwine.

Slithering across the furnace surface, two meet, their patterns different but their skin the same. They glide towards each other and continue, scales sliding and entwining, as they rise higher and higher together, bodies lifted in ecstasy. The defiant boldness of their nature ensures their survival in the barren wilderness, with the fruits of the wild offering themselves up.

13 SHAMAN

Emboldened further by the fire and the intoxication of the wild, The Entwined journey to the blooming meadow to meet with the Shaman. Her song is sung to the beat of Love, and she welcomes the two of the same skin to the skin of her drum; the circle holding the eternal beat. The very beat of Life itself.

Time stands still while the skin of the thinking mind is shed. It takes pause to notice this layer. It takes time to shed; what follows is a step into the eternal.

With the bravery of letting go comes the opening of heart and mind.

The Entwined are bold.

They journey through the Shaman's portal into the Other World.

21 COUNCIL OF ALL BEINGS

The Entwined enter through the portal where the Council of All Beings waits by the Tree of Life and the Waters of Spirit.

Earth, Air, Fire, and Water merge with the Messengers of All, and The Entwined know they have reached the connection of Absolute Home.

The boldness, the bare-faced bones of spirit, the Seeing of the magic in the fire-scorched surroundings others deem as 'barren', has come to fruition. The Entwined can loosen their stance, fully shed the skin of their thinking minds, safe in the knowledge they are Fully Home.

SIX OF FIRE

The Entwined, fully transformed, travel together through the realms, at times touching the precarious, earthly, material plane, where life can feel teetering and bowed under pressure.

But for the two of the same skin, they are always held with and in love, and tread lightly through the earthbound challenges.

Look to the heart and see unwavering Light.

What next for The Entwined, after such an ethereal dance?

FOUR OF FIRE

What's next is Home.

For the connection, the entwining, the journeying, and the victory all lead Home. The persistence, the resilience, the arid heat of the fire magic, the boldness to venture, the willingness to commune...were all worth it.

Home can be experienced in all ways in a rich, nourishing environment.

And so, The Entwined begin their new life.

Angel Boy

0 PILGRIM

She starts across the night-glossed field, stepping lightly through the moonlit hogweed. Pilgrim is ready for the journey. Her heart is lifted by an unseen force whose ethereal beauty glitters in the sky and paves the way for the Pilgrim earth girl.

10 OFFERING

Pilgrim reaches a small copse and stops at a sapling hung with tiny offerings. She feels her heart open as she joins in and offers all she has to hang on the growing sapling – her cord bracelet.

As she ties it with care to the young tree, Pilgrim catches sight of something in her peripheral vision. A boy of the most exquisite beauty watches her as she stumbles to her feet and looks down to the ground, away from the glare of his beauty.

Unable to resist, Pilgrim peeks up through her eyelashes, and her breath almost disappears at the sight of him. His beauty is part of the trees, the birds, the sky, and all the stars beyond. He blends into the cosmos and stands out from it at the same time. He is part of the Earth and all that holds her.

He is ethereal, too far, translucent, untouchable. Her offerings would sink into the dirt and be soaked up by all rooted in it.

Angel Boy appears anchored in the skies even as he shows himself on the earthly realm.

Pilgrim felt her self move ever further the more she tried to reach.

3 SUN

Pilgrim was captivated. She couldn't touch the Angel Boy, but he had touched her. From the moment she had set out on her moonlit journey with her heart open and pure, she had given up her heart, and he held it in his hands inscribed with the language of the Universe.

Her heart was safe with starflower and foxglove in his grasp. He held the roots of the Earth in his touch, and the suns of the cosmos in his body. The sky and all her companions radiated from his skin.

She could never touch him, but he could consume her.

Her Angel Boy.

Elemental

PAGE OF CUPS

The chalice of all things unseen rests on the upturned fingertips of Page of Cups. She touches lightly the vessel that holds the secrets of breath, bone, and heart, stars, seeds, and other worlds.

Deep in the heart of the forest, Page of Cups reads the trees, listens to the moss, and fuses with the cosmos in every second as it lives and dies. All of No Time flows from her chalice, an infinite stream writhing and twisting around her dress.

Ever listening, ever looking, ever seeking, emotions and visions pass to and fro through her skin. A magical membrane. She can feel her blood as cool water, her breath the whisper of breeze through the hawthorn blossoms beyond the forest depths.

She touches the heights of the stars and the depth networks of mycelium and weaves the visions with her fairy fingers.

KNIGHT OF WANDS

Through the network of the forest, Page of Cups feels the arrival of blood heat. It rolls through the woodland like a fiery mist, pure life beat.

Knight of Wands pauses at the edge of the treeline for a fraction of a heartbeat. His mission has led him this far, and he's followed the rhythm of his steed and his blazing heart. A whisper of breath stills him. Stirs him. Beckons him.

His blood heat is genuine. His moment of stilling is just enough to show him the threads running through the forest air. He sets his horse on one of those invisible threads and follows it, infusing the atmosphere with passion. The trees lean towards him, breathing in his intoxicating life fire, flourishing anew in his wake.

Forest spirits dance by the beating hooves, willing Knight of Wands to his destiny.

His energy reaches her first. Page of Cups feels the heat of passion trickle through her membrane, the skin she feels everything with, touches everything with.

In a heartbeat, Knight of Wands is touched. A crash of cool waters floods his body as he looks on Page of Cups. It doesn't act to quench his passion but to wash it clear and pure for him to see with conviction. His destiny blazes before him.

He reaches out trembling fingers, burning with love. "It's you. Elemental girl."

6 LOVERS

Page of Cups and Knight of Wands walk slowly towards each other as whispers of the Universe writhe around them. The forest dissolves in a breath as fingers greet fingers, heartbeat meets heartbeat, fire reacts to water, skin touches, and the transformation of Love begins. Page and Knight merge and morph as they make love inside the watch of angels.

17 STAR

Page of Cups and Knight of Wands, fused as Lovers, burst an orgasm of pure alignment into the Universe. Star, their love child, sits naked amidst an endless sky, an eternal ocean. The breath, skin, heat, and fluid of Love have created a space of magical possibility. True love and passion have cleared the way, and Star has a clear canvas spread before her to paint the magic of infinite inspiration.

Wild Child

TEN OF WANDS

The nine wands glowed with fire in Wild Child's sling as she held aloft the tenth wand to light the way. So many others stooped beneath the weight of passion, suffering, and destiny, refusing to take out the tenth wand and turn it into a starting point.

But Wild Child was not afraid to work with the fire of fear. Looking the lessons in the eye, with the arched brows of defiant knowledge, Wild Child would torch the way into a new wilderness.

QUEEN OF PENTACLES

The new wilderness hosts the throne of the Queen of Pentacles. Her wildness has grown and matured and is firmly rooted in the wild land she presides over. The wildness of the Earth beats its rhythm regardless of what structures and systems are built over it. These cannot last, and the Queen revels in knowing that her wild nature is more real and enduring.

The wildness of the mother is as savage and true as the volcanoes and dirt, the vines and the weeds. Untamed, never unjust. Wild nourishment trumps all table manners.

TEN OF SWORDS

Wild Queen feels the rumble of tame thoughts, the tame thoughts that wind and bind, slowly but surely suffocating the slave who stays in them.

Wild Child, Wild Queen gathers up each thought, each structure, examining each blade as she turns it this way and that in the dim light. Her ferocity gives her firelight to see by. Old blades look fresh to worn eyes, but to those with the untamed strength of vision and boldness, the blades are useful for only one thing.

Slaying that which they enslave.

She picks up the swords one to ten and drives them in to kill the old thought forms and start anew.

The Path

EIGHT OF VISIONS

The woman drifted into The Enchanted Forest and felt herself split into eight versions. The selves drifted here and there, searching and seeking, reaching out to the trees, scrying in the pools, feeling through the mists. All seemed an illusion, but the Enchanted Forest was real. The very thing that was unbelievable was the only trusted thing. The eight seeking selves of the woman simply needed to see through the delusion.

SEVEN OF BOONS

One self put a foot on the heart path and all the other selves amalgamated back into this one. The woman found the path led to seven doors, all set in a huge oak, each one different yet all blending into the mighty tree, the steady Ancient One.

"Which one will you choose?" the Ancient One asked of the woman.

The woman looked, feeling Time disappear for her moment of choice. Each door was a different shade of green, brown, or red, and each held a sigil carved into the wood. Only one door called to her with a song straight from her spirit.

"I choose the green circular door."

The Ancient One creaked as the sigil glowed; the door opened.

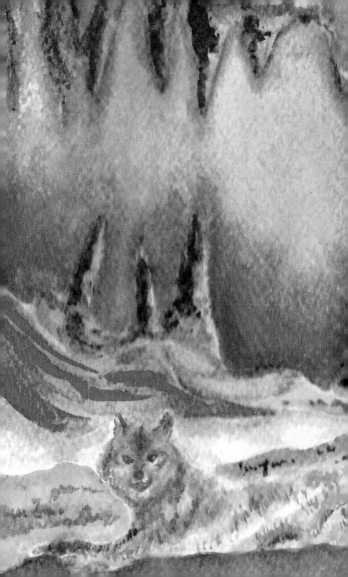

SIX OF BOONS

An inviting room beckoned the woman in. The warmest, softest blankets offered warmth and kindness. Wolves circled, padding the mossy ground for her to rest on. The mother wolf dragged a blanket to the woman, ready to drape over her once she'd lain on the packed, warm moss.

She felt utterly at home, cared for, and surrounded by the largest generosity of spirit she'd ever known.

Whole.

THREE OF BOONS

As she rested, the woman heard a clattering. She lifted her head and saw a kind-looking old woman with sparkling eyes crinkled at the corners in a smile.

"Make a wish, my dear," the wizened one said as she held some herbs aloft a green earthenware bowl.

Make a wish? Make a wish. The woman felt completely at ease with the wizened one looking at her patiently. Little woodland folk were busy in her workspace, bottling potions, hanging herbs to dry, scribing small labels, and sorting jars of all various shapes and sizes.

What would she wish? She thought back to her fractured selves splintering off and the swirling mists of delusion.

There was nothing to wish for. She was exactly where she was meant to be, and

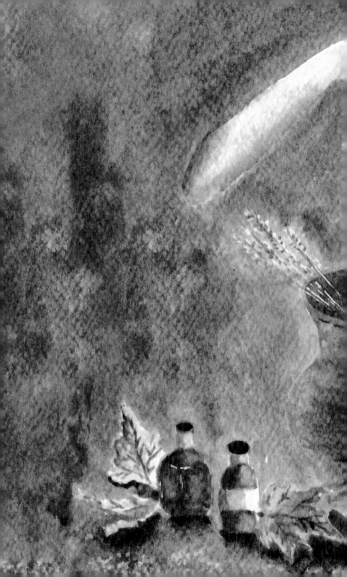

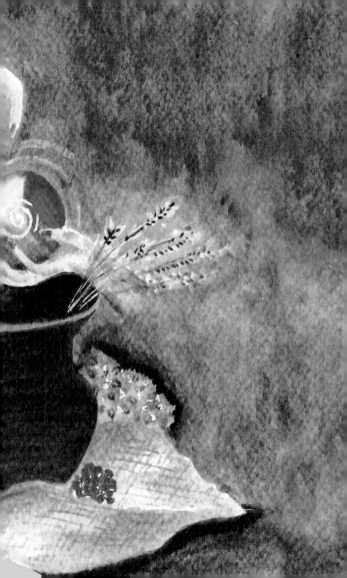

for the first time she could see it with absolute clarity.

The wizened one nodded at her thoughts and scattered the herbs into the bowl with a glittering bang.

"And so it is!"

Dilemma

FIVE OF WANDS

The forest demons surrounded the fly agaric toadstool, their wands blazing like torches. It was the darkness before sunrise, and the flames cast a beautiful light on the lone toadstool.

Fly agaric twisted away from the five demons, uncertain of their intentions, aware that five can be unstable and imbalanced, but her deep, mycellious roots felt a connection with the possibilities this offered.

The demons smelt, tasted, felt Toadstool as they climbed and circled her. The heat from the wands was almost overpowering, it was so close to her fibres. Toadstool sensed the danger, the magic. She sensed the possibility.

She took control of the demons and, tipping her cap to them, made them hers/consumed their fire.

SEVEN OF PENTACLES

After the fire energy of processing the demons, Toadstool needed to earth herself and rest, preparing for further change. Her white stalk transformed into a long dress, her red cap into tresses tumbling down her arms and back, and the white spots little flowers in her hair.

Toadstool had taken the chance. Choosing to transform was not the easy choice. It was the choice of the brave, the choice of one who could take hold of the odds and swing them into their favour.

One can either let the odds take control, or take the energy of instability and turn it into opportunity.

Toadstool slept awhile, watched over by seven trees and nourished from above and below, within and without.

ACE OF CUPS

Toadstool woke feeling renewed and rested. She stretched, yawned, and thanked the seven trees for their protection. Day was breaking, and the laughing caw of a raven split the soft sky. Toadstool looked up to catch the cry, and her heart burst open as Raven met her with the gift of a chalice. The single, shining chalice was placed gently from his talons into her hands.

The fire of the demons was still and clear as she scryed. All creativity seized and stirred in the tumult pooled in the chalice with infinite depth and potential.

All was clear. All was possible. All was to be trusted.

NINE OF CUPS

Toadstool looked long into the chalice, then with a deep breath and a trusting heart, she tossed the chalice up into the air. The silhouette fractured against the pale, blue opening in the trees and rained down nine drops of gold.

Toadstool circled beneath the nine gifts as they fell, her heart and eyes wide open, her arms outstretched.

Nine golden cups orbited her body, spinning and shining in the sunlight. Not one drop of liquid fell but shimmered in each brim-full cup. Toadstool was transfixed by the beauty and stood amidst the nine cups, drinking in the visions each one offered her.

TEN OF CUPS

Toadstool found a clearing outside the forest. A mountain plateau. She planted herself calmly, awaiting the completion of her transformation. After the initial embracing of the danger, the threat, absorbing the fire magic of fear, the alchemy worked swiftly.

A full moon lit the sky as the day came to an end and a fresh start promised.

Ten cups arced overhead, and the glistening droplets kissed Toadstool's head, gently releasing spores from her hair. They drifted in the moonlight, little wisps of glittering life that would become.

Toadstool settled down for the happy ever after.

Acroterium

SEVEN OF CHALLENGES

The vardo window glowed with lamplight cast against orange curtains. Smouldering embers from a fire lit up three foxes as they crept past the caravan door with their booty. The fire tripod held an empty hook, the evidence of a satisfying meal, now being digested in the peace of the travellers' home.

The travellers had come to rest in the heart of the forest. They didn't think of putting down roots; their roots travelled with them. The question was, how much could roots of this nature uphold?

WISE WOMAN

The travellers came out in the morning to an empty camp. The smell of the foxes was pungent and all pervading, and the camp felt full of the ghosts of deception. Treading through the clearing, the travellers followed the scent of lavender and bone, fern and feather.

Wise Woman sat beneath an apple tree and looked up at the two travellers as they stopped in front of her. No words needed to be spoken for her to hear their question.

She cast the bones down onto the ground, a glimpse of sparkle mingling with the feather and bone.

Wise Woman looked at the bones cast, then looked up at the travellers. "The way is clear." Her voice was like running water over river pebbles. "Face the challenge, find the magic, and true stability will uphold all further weight."

TWO OF CHALLENGES

The travellers gathered some apples for their journey, loaded their rucksacks, and tightened their bed rolls. They accepted a small pouch from Wise Woman, fixed it to their belts, and set off. The challenge lay in the forest and was of a different nature to the challenge of deception in the clearing.

The travellers morphed into one as they walked and reached a mirror in the heart of the forest. One became two again as a reflection was suspended mid-air. The travellers faced themselves, two essentially one, one always needing to see two.

Nothing could be supported without confronting this vision Wise Woman had known was waiting. To be protected from deceptions, one must look inside and see what energy supports the self. Air fanned the flames and fire blazed inside.

ACE OF SPELLS

The energy of fire burnt away all external deceptions and toxicity, and the travellers merged and shape-shifted into a dragon living in the heart of the forest – the supporting hearth place for all future spells, for all magic, for all creativity and movement. All was supported in this moment of beginning, this apex.

Belly furnace burning hot and deep.

Trio of creation.

Upholding strength, fire, and magic for all to see.

True Love

KING OF CUPS

Ocean spirits writhed and danced, a foamy conglomerate presided over by King of Cups. With his chalice of vision and his sceptre of emotion, he could stand amidst the churning spirits as they flowed and frothed. To command water was to command the call of the heart, the vision of the all-seeing eye, the storm and toss of emotion.

King of Cups felt the wrangle and writhe of the water spirits beneath his blue body, his aqua eyes piercing the multiple layers as they shifted and flowed. Two dolphins leapt. King of Cups felt them before they breached, momentarily out of the waves. Two spirits free and joined, they fell back into the ocean.

SEVEN OF CUPS

King of Cups saw the connection between the two dolphin spirits in his kingdom of emotion. Their clarity shone through the waters like a vision. King of Cups called Magician to make an offering of choice to the two water spirits. How best to work with the magic of this true connection? How best to unify in the face of vast emotions and energies?

Magician rose above the waters, his pointed hat reaching into the perfect clouds scudding the blue sky. Seven chalices, each one filled with a possibility, hovered in front of him, sustained by his gesture of offering.

Seven chalices; seven visions; seven choices.

One chalice burst with vivid fruit and flowers; a second held an entire cosmos; the third was bursting with a verdant forest, the smell of pine mingling with the salt foam that sprayed from the fourth cup. Two people sat across a café table in the fifth cup, steaming mugs of coffee either side of a vase of freesia, two hands stretched across the table, fingers entwined like growing ivy. The sixth chalice held an ouroboros, kundalini energy sparkling, in wait for that biting spark to ignite.

The final and seventh cup carried a bright spring day. Blue sky emanated from the chalice; the aroma of grass and earth, fresh breeze and crocus wafted from within. Three trees grew on the hill that rose out of the goblet, a perfect mound of fertile earth supporting the three ancient lives.

KNIGHT OF SWORDS

Surrounded by the sea of emotion and vision, the two spirits were entranced by such offerings. The possibilities called, and the mind was tossed on the waves, drowning in the heart.

The two heart spirits felt a clean pull up from the threat of immersion as the crisp slice of a blade cut through the air. Knight of Swords charged along the beach, his pristine sword held aloft. The clarity of the sword cut through any turbulence that endless possibility had churned up.

The boundaries were clear. The mission was clear. The aim was crystal sharp and full of precise passion.

TWO OF CUPS

The vigour, clarity, and passion of Knight of Swords carved the shape of the water spirits as they thanked the Magician and chose their chalice.

A crash of waves washed them to a clear, bright shore. The ouroboros encircled the two Lovers as they merged and morphed, becoming the very energy that encircled them.

The kundalini energy rose as old skin was sloughed off with each mouthful, a continuous cycle of rebirthing each moment, of giving and taking, of uniting, of becoming and losing.

The hill with the three trees rose in the background, waiting for the Lovers to retire there in all eternity. Extra blessings can be offered when one is grasped with an open and honest heart.

True love opens all possibilities.

Persistence, or The Cost of Peace

DEVIL

Fear, angst, rage, and toil morphed and grew before the young warrior's eyes. A great, red beast drew power from the feed that was a seed of uncertainty. The young warrior breathed deep into his belly, keeping his gaze fixed on the devil, watching the length of chain in his clawed hand. The links were forged from particles of anger, hatred, fear, anxiety.

The warrior paused. Did the devil bear the chains? Or did he wield them?

The young warrior recognised every single link in the chain; he recognised every fibre of fur sprouting on the devil's skin. Each hair grew from a foundation of fear, a memory the warrior craved to smash. He drew back his sword, poised to smite the devil down.

The flames from the fire flickered and cast a new light on the red beast.

The warrior pointed his sword to the flames and looked the devil straight in the eyes. He saw himself in all his furious glory.

He stepped forward.

ACE OF WANDS

Holding aloft the flame, the young warrior stepped into the devil. His sword had transformed into a wand, and the power burned bright as the links in the chain disintegrated to ashes, the fur on the red skin blackened to a crisp.

"Where do we go from here, now that we've grown?"

SIX OF PENTACLES

The devil and the young warrior merged, shifted, and split into two young girls. Their skin was pure, their eyes bright, and their hair hung long down their backs. A horned beast dropped an abundance of golden coins into one girl's hands, whilst the other girl tattooed their names across the beast's heart.

The tripod of figures was doubled by six pentacles framing their outline. The beast's voice whispered through the air like wind stroking pussy willow. "Now you've accepted the power of beasts, the world is yours to reap."

SIX OF WANDS

It was a glorious moment. Six wands were ignited as Peace journeyed, victorious over the monsters that had previously haunted her. In swaddling cloths she carried Future, who suckled at her breast and was admired by the attendants who accompanied Peace.

forever

5 OF EARTH

Mother Hare leapt over the clover, feeling the bones of her ancestors beneath her, clodded by the red earth. A nest of babies snuggled close to the old bones, the warmth of the earth seeping in and around their bodies. The beat of the Earth matched the beat of their hearts, and Mother Hare relished the hum of the cycle.

Life and death. Death and rebirth. Circles and cycles of creation.

Always.

She pined for the Earth to feel it.

4 OF EARTH

Mother Hare crossed the clover and into the place of the standing stones.

"You know the continual cycles," she whispered to the stones.

Their energy stretched from the tips to the outer reaches of the cosmos. From the base to the very centre core of the planet.

Their stability was unceasing, endless, eternal. They saw and felt All.

Mother Hare went to sit in the centre of the standing stones. The buzz of balanced energy crackled through to the tips of her furs. Mother Hare, the great conductor of creation, willed the fruition and sweetness far and wide.

3 OF EARTH

It rippled through the grasses; it moved through the soil; it cast on the breeze; it travelled through the roots; it transformed through animal cells.

And all the land and her offspring bloomed with fertility, a fertility of union and creativity.

Mother Hare still felt the bones of ancestors below, felt the spirit above, below, and beyond, within and without.

"But what of the death?" the horses asked.

"But what of the endings?" the cows asked.

"But what of the cycles?" the birds asked.

The people were silent.

Mother Hare listened to the questions and despaired of the silence.

She sprang up to the top of the hillside amongst the bluebells and the yarrow and looked out over the blooming land.

"Listen carefully, one and all, the death, the endings, the cycles are all part of the never-ending creation. This is what makes the eternal roll of forever. Do not dwell on the nature of endings and death as a full stop, but as a crest of a wave that is eternally unfolding and unfolding."

10 OF WATER

As she spoke, the skies let go of their water and the planet bloomed with enormous leaves, vines, thick roots, and tendrils. Animals emerged from the soil, from behind gnarly trunks, from beneath the umbrella of leaves. A chorus of birds chattered resonant echoes through the lush forest of green and rain.

The purr of big cats, the hum of insects, the growl of wolves swept over the land, through the skies, deep into the molecules of the soil. The planet was lush, full of rich life that would forever loop with completion and birthing.

Mother Hare watched the flourishing planet in all her natural glory before being swallowed in a mouthful of thick, terracotta earth, her fur, teeth, and bones absorbed into the clay, her spirit dispersed in the droplets of water, forever cycling through the planet, forever free in the grand cosmos.

End…

About the Author

Diane King is from Buxton, a spa town in the English Peak District, where she has found many characters and stories on its hillsides, up its trees and in its strange pools. She hopes you love reading those stories as much as she loves writing them.

To find out more about Diane's stories, visit:
https://www.diane-king.com

Beaten Track Publishing

For more titles from Beaten Track
Publishing,
please visit our website:

https://www.beatentrackpublishing.com

Thanks for reading!

Printed in Great Britain
by Amazon